At Mary Bloom's

written and illustrated by **ALIKI**

Greenwillow Books | A Division of William Morrow & Company, Inc., New York

E
Ali

Library of Congress Cataloging in Publication Data: Aliki. At Mary Bloom's.
Summary: Relates what happens at Mary Bloom's when her friend's mouse has babies.
I.   Title   PZ7.A397At   [E]   75-45482   ISBN 0-688-80048-3   ISBN 0-688-84048-5 lib. bdg.
ISBN 0-688-02480-7 (1983 Printing)   ISBN 0-688-02481-5 (lib. bdg.: 1983 Printing)

For Mary
and Alexa,

who made it happen

My mouse just had babies!
I'll go tell Mary Bloom.

But if I do,
I know what will happen.

Her bell will ring

the baby will cry

the dogs will bark

the cat will escape

the owl will shiver

the skunk will shake

the magpie will call

the monkey will shriek

the hamsters will hide

the gerbil will race

the rabbit will twitch

and her mice
won't like it either.

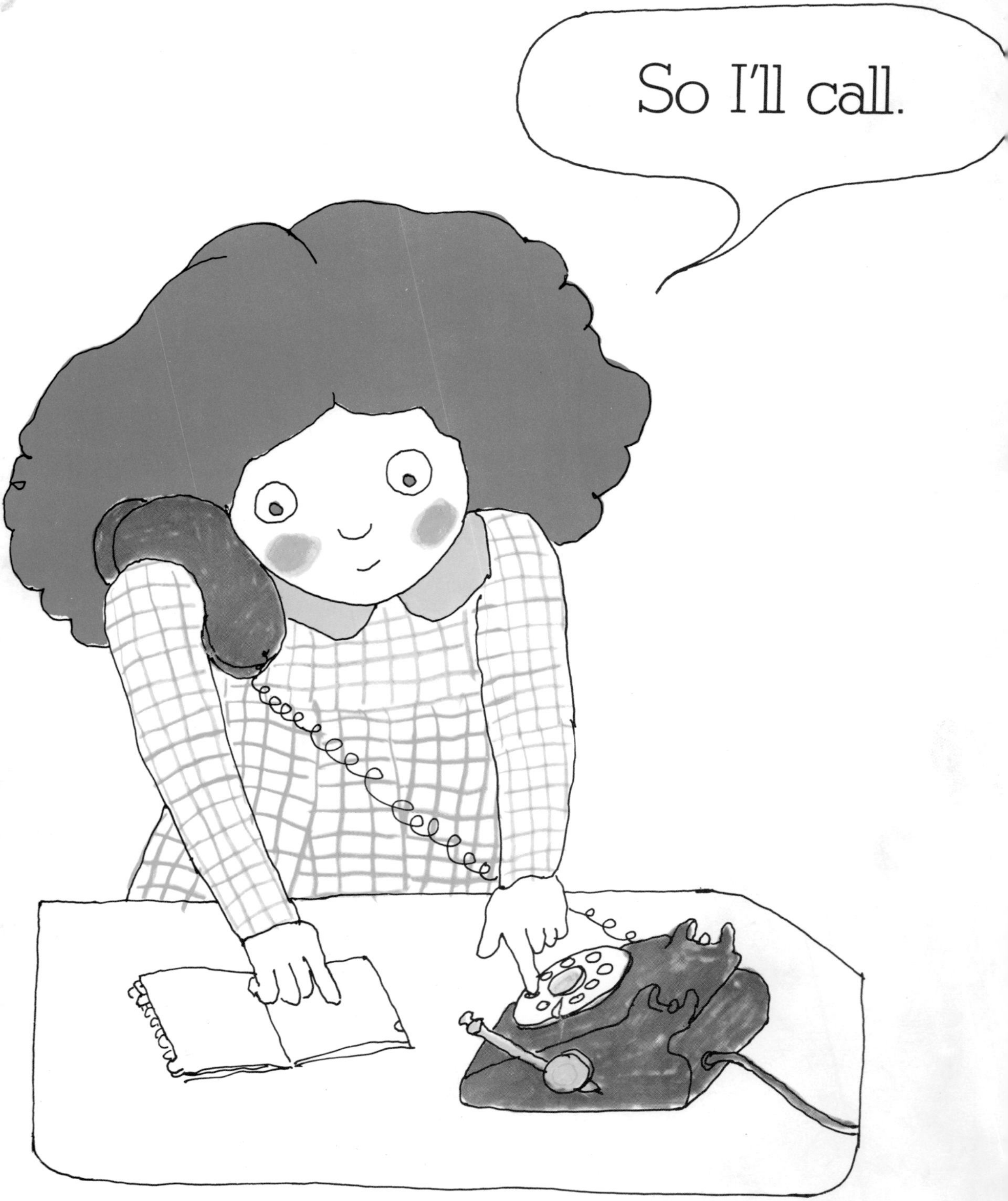
So I'll call.

At Mary Bloom's
the telephone rang
the baby cried
the dogs barked
the cat escaped
the owl shivered
the skunk shook
the magpie called
the monkey shrieked
the hamsters hid
the gerbil raced
the rabbit twitched
and her mice
didn't like it either.

MIDDLEBURY ELEMENTARY SCHOOL
MEDIA CENTER

So I rang her bell.

But  the baby didn't cry

the dogs didn't bark

the cat didn't escape

the owl didn't shiver

the skunk didn't shake

the magpie didn't call

the monkey  didn't shriek

the hamsters  didn't hide

the gerbil didn't race

the rabbit didn't twitch

and her mice
didn't seem to mind.

They were expecting me.

So the baby
and the dogs
the cat
the owl
the skunk
the magpie
the monkey
the hamsters
the gerbil
the rabbit
her mice
and I...

celebrated at Mary Bloom's

the day my mouse had babies.

the end